For Lainey-loulou, Tombo and the Edster

.

The Mysterious

Neighbours at Number 33

ISBN: 978-1-9165009-1-4

Vampires

The story you are about to read is about vampires. And it is a true story!

I know you think that I am lying. You think vampires are the stuff of fairy-tales. That they're make believe, like fairies, unicorns, dragons, or teachers with a sense of humour. But you are wrong. Dead wrong! Vampires are real! And while most of you reading this will probably never encounter one, they are out there, hiding in the shadows of villages, towns and cities across the world.

So, before I begin the story, I feel I must give you some information on vampires. You need to know their habits and what makes them tick. And most importantly, you need to know how you can protect yourself, should you ever come across one! I couldn't bear it if you were only two chapters into this book and discovered that a vampire was living nearby and didn't know what to do. So, I beg you, please read the following chapters very carefully. This information could one day save your life!

I will begin with a fact that you probably already know - that vampires drink blood. But what you can't imagine is how much they *crave* it. Vampires have a thirst for blood that is unimaginable to you or I. Cast your mind back to the time when you were the thirstiest you've ever been. I should imagine it was during a long, hot summer's day after you had been foolishly running around with your friends. You were probably dripping in sweat and had a face the colour of an embarrassed strawberry. Do you remember how your throat felt like the skin of a cactus being scraped by rough sandpaper? And do you recall how good that drink felt as it slipped down your throat? It may have been an ice cold can of your favourite fizzy pop, it could have been a freshly squeezed orange juice in a tall tumbler, or it might have been a glass of ordinary tap water, but whatever it was, that feeling you had when you guzzled that drink was one of complete joy. A vampire feels a thirst stronger than this all of the time, and they only get the sensation of total refreshment when that rich cherry blood passes their pale lips.

So you can understand why they want it so badly!

Now, I tell you this as I want you to realise something - if you come across a vampire, they will want to drain you of every drop of your precious blood. You will not be able to reason with the creature, plead with it, or beg for mercy. There are but two choices - you run for your life, or you kill the vampire. Failing in this will lead to only one outcome....your untimely death!

By this point, you may have noticed that when I talk of vampires I use the word *it,* and not he, or she. That's because vampires aren't human. Despite looking human in many ways, vampires are actually a totally different species altogether. Vampires actually share more genetic similarities with bats than people. And this is why they are similar in many ways. For example, they only come out at night, they both have fangs, they both drink blood and they both have little furry pig faces. Actually, come to think of it, the last one usually only refers to bats. Anyway, vampires and bats are *so* alike that a vampire can shapeshift into a bat at will. Being able to turn into a bat means that a vampire can travel large distances in a short space of time and can enter most houses at ease, either by flying through a gap in an open window or by flying down the chimney. So I'm sorry to inform you of this girls and boys, but while a chimney is useful for the big guy to come down at Christmas, it is also lethal if you have a vampire living nearby!

The final thing I can tell you about vampires is that they have no reflection.

So, it is fairly safe to assume that Justin Bieber is not a vampire!

But everyone else - unless you have seen them in the daylight, or you have seen their reflection, be on your guard. They could very well be a vampire!

How to Protect Yourself from a Vampire Attack

So now you better understand what a vampire is, it's now time to find out what you can do if you ever come across one. I urge you to take out a pencil and make notes here, because this information is vital!

Now I'm not going to lie to you, if you ever come face to face with a vampire then you are in deep doo-doo. But there are things you can do to protect yourself from vampires and help prevent yourself from becoming their next meal!

You've already learned that vampires can turn into bats, which helps them enter your house to feast on your blood, so it makes sense to shut your windows at night. Unfortunately vampires are crafty, so it doesn't mean that if you have all your windows bolted you will definitely be sleeping safe and sound in the morning. But closing your windows certainly helps. Leaving your windows open not only allows vampires easy access into your bedroom, it also releases the scent of your blood into the air, which can attract nearby vampires.

To vampires, humans are like crisps - we are all flavoured differently. Each blood type gives off a slightly different scent, and while they are certainly not fussy, their favourite flavor is O positive. So if this is your blood type, then closing your windows at night is a must!

But even if you are in the unfortunate position of having O positive blood, there is still something you can do to put a vampire off eating you.

Vampires don't like garlic. It smells utterly putrid to them. And, as I'm sure you are aware, if you eat garlic, then you stink of garlic. So if you have had a large helping of garlic recently, then this may be enough to put a vampire off eating you. Imagine a scenario where a vampire breaks into your house and enters the bedroom that you share with a sibling. Well, if you tucked into a chicken kiev for tea, while your brother or sister had fish fingers and chips, then the chances are that the vampire would ignore you and munch on them instead. Result!

But gobbling garlic will only get you so far. If a vampire goes a few days without drinking blood, they become even more ravenous than normal. So hungry in fact, that they would still eat you, even if you had eaten garlic for breakfast, lunch and dinner. Think about it. What would you do if you were starving and got a burger from McDonald's but it had a gherkin on top? You would just peel off the slimy critter and eat the burger anyway, right? It may spoil the flavour a bit, but I bet you would still eat it.

At this point, I know what you're thinking - that all these little tips may help protect you to a degree, but they aren't guaranteed to save you! And you're right. And here is where I have some good news and some bad news for you. The good news is there are a few ways to kill a vampire.

The bad news is, none of them are easy.

The first thing to be aware of is that vampires cannot go out in the daylight.

Do you know a horrible boy? You may be a horrible boy yourself? Either way, I'm sure you have heard of horrible boys who pour salt onto slugs. When the salt hits the skin of a slug it causes a chemical reaction that turns their sleek bodies into a mass of sticky ooze. It's disgusting. And it's also excruciatingly painful for the slug. Now, when the Ultra Violet (UV) rays of the sun hit the skin of a vampire, it has the exact same effect. After just seconds in the sun, a vampire's skin will begin to bubble and smoke, and in no time at all, the creature will turn to dust.

Sadly, this isn't all that helpful. The only way you could kill a vampire this way is by breaking into its house during the daytime, when it's asleep, before pulling open the curtains to let the sunshine blare in. You would then have to prize open the vampire's coffin to expose it to the sunlight. But vampires aren't stupid. They purposely sleep in thick coffins that are locked securely from the inside, usually in a room with no windows. So, I would not recommend entering a vampire's house to attempt this, for if you do, you would very likely become their midnight snack (well actually, their midday snack - I suppose).

Probably the best way to destroy a vampire is by soaking them with holy water. When the pure goodness of holy water comes into contact with the evil skin of a vampire, it has a similar effect to sunlight. Even a tiny drop of holy water will cause a bad burn to a vampire and a good soaking will undoubtedly lead it to perish. You can get holy water in any church. It is in the font by the front door. So keep going, day after day, until you have enough to fill a decent sized bottle and then keep this at your bedside at all times. It may be the wisest thing you will ever do.

There are a few more ways to kill a vampire. A stake through the heart, being shot by a silver bullet, or having its head cut off will all destroy the ghastly beast. But a word of warning here - if you suspect someone of being a vampire, please make sure you are one hundred percent sure before slaying them using one of these methods, as they are also known to effectively kill humans. Please don't plunge a stake through your teacher's chest just because he has large canine teeth that are a bit sticky-outy, as more than likely, you wouldn't have killed a vampire - you would have just committed murder!

So now you are in possession of all of the facts. Chances are you will never need this information as vampires are an extremely rare species. But then you never know, there could be a vampire living on your very street!

MISSING

Mr E. Wright

Last seen 2nd August
Any informtion ring 0123456789

The Mysterious Neighbours at Number 33

They stole in under the cover of darkness, like sneak thieves. Their car wheels were barely turning as they ever-so-slowly crept up the road to number 33. The headlights were off. It was as if they didn't want to disturb anyone. But I heard them. And when I peeked through the curtains of my bedroom window, I saw them too. One man and one woman. I think anyway, it was hard to tell being so dark. They unpacked the car in no time. They hardly had anything - just two wooden boxes of luggage that they slid out of the boot upon arrival.

They opened the front door, hauled in the boxes and that was it. That was the last time that I had seen them.

It had now been fourteen days - a fortnight - two weeks (take your pick) and if it wasn't for the silver estate that sat stationary in the drive, you would never have known anyone had actually moved in. The faded mustard drapes, that had somehow appealed to the previous owners, had not yet been replaced and were drawn tight across every window. The sold sign, displaying the estate agent's cheesy grin, still remained propped up against the fence and the grass inched taller by the day.

It was all very strange and rumours among the neighbourhood children had begun to spiral out of control. Some said they were werewolves. Some believed them to be vampires. A few thought them to be fiends or murderers. Others suggested they were in witness protection or that they were undercover secret agents, or spies. You name it, every kid had an explanation for it. My best friend Sean was the worst. He had a different theory for every day of the week. Mind you, he always had a wild imagination. He even told me once that his cousin Eddie used to have a baby T-rex as a pet. His brother, Mark, who had just walked into Sean's room uninvited, was just as bad.

"I'm surprised to see you here, Tom. I'm surprised you are even still alive to be honest, what with those new neighbours of yours. They're right weirdos them."

He was a fine one to talk. You see, Mark had recently become a goth. Or he had become an emo. I'm not sure? But either way, he was dark. He wore all black now - baggy black jumpers, black jeans that were *so* tight that it looked like his bare legs had been coated in black paint and clunky black boots. His eyes were framed by a thin layer of messy black eyeliner and he had recently dyed his wild back-combed hair black, even though his natural hair colour was already a very dark brown. The only thing not black about Mark was the army of angry red spots that had taken to marching across his face over the past year or so.

"Get lost, Mark," said Sean.

"I'm not called Mark anymore, you normo! I'm called Deadly Nightshade now, and you'll do well to remember that!" he said, waving his hands over Sean, as if to cast an evil enchantment over him.

"I saw them you know. When I had a sleep over at Draven's house the other night, I saw them digging in the garden. It was half past two in the morning and they were digging a huge hole. Six foot deep, at least. And when they had digged it, they threw something big in it. It took both of them to lift it. Now what might that be?"

"A dead body!" said Sean, managing to follow the trail of huge breadcrumbs that his brother had just scattered on the floor in front of him.

"A dead body is right!" said Mark. "I reckon they're murderers. It was them that killed that guy whose gone missing. You know, the guy on all those posters around town!"

"I knew it, I knew it," said Sean, standing from the bed and flapping his arms like a disco dancing pigeon. "I knew they were murderers."

Although Sean now wholeheartedly believed that murderers were living in the neighbourhood, I wasn't as easily convinced. Mark had a history of telling tall tales and I suspected that this was just the latest in a long list of wind ups. "Hang on a minute, have you got any proof of all this? How about you take us over to Draven's house and let us see out of the window for ourselves?"

Draven Grey, whose real name was Brian Warner, lived three doors down from me. He was one of only two residents on Sange Drive that had a decent view of the new neighbours' back garden. I, like all the other houses on the street, could see the front perfectly, but the back garden was a more exclusive club. As number 33 was at the end of the cul-de-sac, only the next door neighbours had that privilege.

"Proof is it?" said Mark. He then squeezed his hand into his tiny pocket and rummaged around. A lot of huffing and puffing followed, but at last Mark managed to wrestle free his phone from his jeans. A few quick flicks of his finger across the screen and then the phone was held up, right in front of our faces. And there it was. There was the proof. A photo of a patch of lawn with a large mound of freshly dug up earth sitting on top.

Sean was aghast. "Well, they're definitely murderers then. I'm ten out of ten percent sure of that. So what are we going to do about it?"

"I'm not going to *do* anything," said Mark, casually. "Death is natural. It's part of the circle of life."

I'd always thought that Mark was cool. Older kids are always cooler than us younger kids anyway, and being fifteen made Mark four years cooler than me. But to be honest, Mark had got a bit annoying since he turned goth, or emo.

"I'll leave you to figure this one out for yourselves," said Mark. "I'm off to feed Robert Smith now, mortals. Goodbye."

And off he went to feed dead crickets to Robert Smith, his bearded dragon. It was only six months ago that the spiky reptile was still called Godzilla. But when Mark turned goth, seemingly so did his pet, and so he was now named after the lead singer of some dreary gothic band called, the Cure. Mark staggered zombie-like across the landing toward his room. He placed his hand on the door handle and yanked it open. Instantly the smell burst free. It was the stench of stale sweat and cheap incense sticks. The strong musty smell that only a teenage boy's cave could make. Mark entered his dungeon, slamming the door behind him.

"Well he's obviously not going to do anything, so what are *we* going to do?" said Sean, as miserable music began to seep like a poisonous fog through the walls of Mark's room.

I shrugged my shoulders. "I'm sure there's probably some reasonable explanation for it all," I said, sounding almost like I believed it, "but here's an idea - why don't we have a sleep over at my house tonight and we can stake out their house. We can't see the back garden, but I have a good view of the front. And then, if any weird stuff *is* happening, we will hopefully see it with our own eyes."

"Sounds like a plan," agreed Sean. Suddenly his facial expression turned extremely serious.

I thought it was to do with all the strangeness at number 33. But it wasn't.

"Now, let's discuss something very important - snacks! I'll bring around a bag of jellies, some popcorn, nachos and dip, a multi-pack of crisps, some marshmallows, a tub of

11

chocolates, a few packets of biscuits, a bag of lollies and a couple of big bottles of coke. But will you try and get some stuff too? We don't want to be left short."

I nodded. But I knew that no matter how much there was to eat that Sean wouldn't be left short, although I most certainly would be.

The Stay Awake Over

It was a perfect night for a stake out. There wasn't a cloud in the sky and the moon shone big and bright above the street, like a torch waiting to flash its light over anything out of the ordinary. Sean was a bag of nerves as he thought it was a full moon and anticipated werewolves. I knew better. While the moon looked full, it was actually a waxing gibbous moon. And that is a real thing - check if you don't believe me!

But so far it had all been a total waste of time. We had been watching the neighbours' house since dusk fell and nothing of interest had happened at all. We had not left the window once - well actually, we had left it once, while we played on the PlayStation downstairs, but that was only for an hour - and not even a single light had been turned on. It was now creeping up to two in the morning and I was getting more bored and tired with each passing second.

"This is pointless. There's nothing happening. When can we go to bed?"

"Look, there's still a small bit of food left, so let's finish that and then, if there is still nothing happening, we can hit the hay," said Sean, cramming yet another marshmallow into his already jam packed gob. Sean's ability to eat was truly amazing. The effortless ease in which a black hole devours entire solar systems was nothing compared to when food was placed in front of him. And yet, he was as skinny as a rake. I had asked Sean once why he never put on weight. He said he had good genes that helped keep him slim, and I knew that this was the reason he had decided to wear his finest denim pants for tonight's midnight feast.

"Okay, another half an hour then," I squeezed out in a yawn. My eyes were all dry and I could feel my eyelids getting heavier and heavier and heavier, as if there were two small weights on them pushing them down. So I stretched them open to prevent them from closing. And that's when I noticed something.

"Sean, what's that?"

"What's what?" Sean mumbled, pushing the final marshmallow into a tiny pocket of space in his mouth.

"Out there. Look."

I pressed my face tightly against the window to get a better glimpse into the street. Sean quickly followed suit. And suddenly my eyes didn't feel tried any more. They were wide awake again as I scanned up and down the road to see if I could see it again. And then I did see it again - two small black shadows flashed across my eye line. The figures, illuminated by the glow of the street lamps that lined the street, bounced around the sleepy cul-de-sac like yo-yos on a string, before darting up to the rooftop of number 33, where they shot down the spindly brick chimney at speed.

Immediately, we both peeled back from the window and looked at each other.

"BATS!" we said at exactly the same time. Well, I think we both said bats. It was hard to tell exactly what Sean said with his mouth full of gluey marshmallow.

Sean swallowed hard. "Of course, they're vampires!" he said, before tearing open a huge bag of crisps and shovelling a fistful into the huge hole in his face.

"Vampires? Don't be daft," I said, secretly knowing that he was probably right.

"Well how else do you explain it?" asked Sean. Without waiting even a fraction of a second for my response, he continued. "They're vampires for sure. They must have just returned from hunting. I've heard about this. At night time, vampires turn into bats and go off to find a victim - you see, they can get into people's houses easier when they are bats. Then, once they have had their fill of blood, they return home and get into their coffins before the sun rises."

"How come you're a vampire expert all of a sudden?" I asked.

"I just am," Sean said confidently. "Look, I think that's proof enough that the new neighbours are vampires. The question is, what are we going to do about it?"

I shook my head in disbelief. I tried to think, but my head was all fuzzy. Surely this couldn't be happening here on Sange Drive. Nothing ever happened on Sange Drive, let alone something strange and altogether mysterious. There must be some reasonable explanation for it all. But as I sat there thinking of what this reasonable explanation could be, the front door to the neighbours' house, that had been shut tight since they moved in, slowly crept open. From the doorway a tall thin shadow emerged and sloped gracefully across the front lawn towards the bins at the side of the house. In its hand was a large sack.

Sean and I sat completely still, and watched, as the figure flipped open the top of one of the bins and tossed in the bag. The silhouetted man then returned the lid to the bin and stopped for a moment to look around, before heading back into the house.

"Is that proof enough for you?" asked Sean, spluttering crisp crumbs all over my bedroom floor.

"Okay, that is also a bit weird," I said.

"A bit weird? That's super-weird more like," said Sean. "Who puts out their bins at two in the morning? A vampire, that's who! That rubbish bag is probably full of all vampire stuff."

"What vampire stuff?" I asked.

"I dunno. Body parts, maybe?" said Sean, who despite being in bit of a frenzy, clearly hadn't lost his appetite.

"Hang on, Mark said that they buried a dead body in the garden, so why would they be putting body parts in a bin?"

"Look, I don't claim to be a vampire expert, but something weird is clearly going on here," said Sean. "I just know that if we check the contents of that bin there will be some strange stuff in there. Now let's go out there and have a look," he said, sweeping a fine layer of crisp dust from his lap.

"Wait a minute," I said. "If they are vampires, which I still don't believe they are, but if they are, we don't want to be out on their front lawn looking through their bins in the middle of the night, do we? Not unless we want to be their next victims. No, we wait until first light and have a peek in the bin then." I paused, to try and catch up with my thoughts that were racing further and further away from me. "So shall we try and get some sleep and set the alarm to go off in a couple of hours, or will we just wait up?"

"We wait up!" snapped Sean. "All this vampire stuff has given me the heebie-jeebies. I couldn't sleep now, even if I tried."

It may have been the heebie-jeebies, but I actually suspected that the caffeine from the four litres of coke that Sean had drank may have more to do with his jitters.

"Right then," continued Sean, "we stay up and watch for any more strange going-ons." He paused for a moment. "Is going-ons a word?"

I shook my head. "Going-ons is actually two words. But no, I'm not sure it is a commonly used saying, if that's what you mean?"

Sean nodded. It may not be a common saying, but there was indeed some strange going-ons at number 33 and Sean was sure that it was due to vampires. I was trying to convince myself that it could all be sensibly explained, but I too found myself wondering if it really could be true – I mean, the strangeness was becoming overwhelming. Neighbours that are never seen in the day, the night time digging, bats flying down their chimney and putting out the rubbish when no one is around to see them. All signs were beginning to point to vampirism for sure. Anyway, we would surely soon find out. It was only a short while until sunrise, and then maybe the contents of the bin would clarify the situation once and for all!

The Bin Check

It was just before 6. a.m. The blood red rim of the large early-morning sun had just poked up over the horizon, casting a glorious blanket of pink over the entire street. I know boys aren't supposed to like pink, but I secretly did. The birds were chirping brightly and the air was already warm and heavy, promising so much for the day ahead. But I was in no mood to admire the beautiful summer morn. We had business to attend to!

"You do it," said Sean.

"Why me? Why don't you do it?" I replied.

"Because, I did the last job," said Sean, with a frown.

The last job was walking down the stairs last night to fetch the last bottle of coke. I didn't even get to drink any of it, and even if I did, completing that task was hardly in the same league as this. But I didn't fancy being out on the street longer than we needed to be, so I decided it best not to argue. Sean never listened to reason anyway.

So here I stood on my doorstep, about to embark on my - perhaps dangerous - mission. The neighbours' bin wasn't too far away. Two houses down and then a short sprint across the front lawn was all. But to me it felt like a million miles away. I had thought about creeping up to the bin in stages, using the neighbourhood trees, cars and shrubbery as cover to shield myself, but I had now settled on running over as fast as I could. I just wanted to get it done as quickly as possible. So I put my left foot in front of my right and hunched my back, ready to sprint away.

And that's when Sean chirped in, "They would have put that bag in the black bin."

I looked at him.

"The blue bin is just for paper and plastic. Body parts can't be recycled, they have to go to the dump."

I tell you, there should be a book written about Sean, detailing the ridiculous things that frequently came out of his mouth. It would surely be a best seller!

Meanwhile, my nerves were building by the second. The butterflies that had been fluttering around inside my tummy had seemingly been eaten by crows. A murder of wild pecking crows. Perhaps a rather appropriate name for them, given the current circumstances. I felt my head beginning to swim. The panic growing. I tried to control it, tried to breathe, tried to reassure myself that everything would be alright, but nothing seemed to help. So I decided to just set off.

I ran as fast as I could down my front garden path, past number 29 and number 31 and over the lawn of number 33 to the side of the house, where the bins stood. I placed my trembling hand on the handle and lifted the lid. As it flipped backwards, I could instantly see that the bin was full of black sacks. It seemed the new neighbours had been busy!

Immediately I began tearing at the rubbish bags, spilling the contents out all over the place. Rummaging through the trash uncovered a variety of items presumably left by the previous owners: dusty lampshades, a broken picture frame, a toilet brush stained a worrying shade of brown - but no body parts! I was just about to give up, when I found something of interest buried deep at the bottom of one of the black sacks.

I yanked the frilly night dress up from under the waste and held it up. And that's when things took a turn for the scarier. The snow white dress was stained with large blotches of deep cherry red.

 I waved my hands at Sean to beckon him over.
He ambled over the grass to join me at the
bins.

"Sean, look at this," I said.

"Holy cow, a blood stained nightie!" said Sean. "I bet it belonged to that man that's missing. The man that they killed!"

"Yeah, maybe. But it would probably more likely belong to a woman, wouldn't it?" I said.

A look of wonder spread across Sean's face, like butter being spread over warm toast. "Oh yeah, you're right, it probably does belong to a woman. You know what that means don't you? They've killed that man, and they've also killed a woman - they're serial killers!"

As Sean spoke these words, a shiver rippled over my skin like a cold ocean wave. "I don't like this, Sean. I don't like this one bit. Let's get out of here!"

At once, I dropped the night dress, darted away from the bin and began bolting towards home. But I stopped on the pavement and turned back when I sensed that Sean was not with me. "Sean, come on! Leave the dress and let's go!"

"It's not the dress," replied Sean, who was now half submerged in the neighbours' bin. "There's a pizza box in here, and I don't think it's been opened. I'm just...trying to reach it."

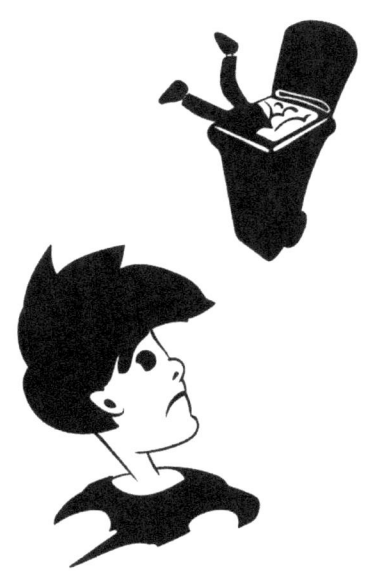

"Forget the pizza. There's a margarita in my freezer. I'll cook it for you back at home."

"But…. this one is Hawaiian," groaned Sean, who looked agonisingly at the pizza wedged in at the bottom of the bin.

"Look, I'll put some fruit on the one I have," I begged, trying to hurry Sean on the best I could. "I haven't got any pineapple but I do have some satsumas. Just please, hurry up!"

Sean found his way out of the bin. Then he flipped the lid back over and made his way over to me. Quickly, we scurried back to my house.

 We had only been on our mission for a few minutes - five max - but when we got back into my house it felt different from when I left it. It no longer felt safe, like a home should. And I

feared that it was only going to get worse from
here on in.

Miss Mangle and
Mr Tibbles

After a seriously intense conversation over some citrus flavoured pizza, we had finally calmed down to the point where we felt just about brave enough to leave the house again. You see the sun was well and truly up now and its common knowledge that vampires cannot go out in daylight. Especially this daylight! It was another scorcher of a day. Sometimes August can usher in an early start to autumn, but not this year. Summer was still very much in full swing, with each day as glorious as the last. The sky was a crystal clear blue with not a wisp of a cloud to be seen. It was still a couple of hours until midday but it was already sweltering. Little beads of sweat were gathering on the nape of my neck and behind my knees as we took it in turns to kick the ball at each other in a penalty shoot-out competition. I was up next. Despite the unmerciful heat, I sprinted up to the ball and smashed it low and hard, like my Dad had taught me, just inside one of the two jumpers that we were using for goal posts.

"That's 3-0. You need to score this one or I win," I said, making my way into the mouth of the goal.

"But it's not fair, I can't concentrate," said Sean.

It was always the same with Sean. There was always some excuse. Last week he had lost because he was concerned about the unusually large ratio of blue smarties in the tube he had bought. This worried Sean because he knew that a few years ago the blue smarties had vanished from smartie tubes and been replaced by white ones. Three years later they returned. The official explanation was that the old blue smarties contained artificial colourings, which were making kids hyper, and they had to find a natural alternative before they brought them back to market. But Sean never believed this. Sean believed that the government spent the three years developing a new blue smartie shell that contained mind control chemicals. No doubt a theory developed by Mark, who seemed to have a much stronger control over Sean's mind than a blue smartie ever could. Anyway, Sean couldn't have been too worried about it, he still ate all the blue smarties. Yes, there was always an excuse with Sean. At least today there was a proper one.

"What are we going to do about the vampires?" fretted Sean.

"Well," I said, "we have four options as I see it. We can tell our parents, but they would never believe us and they would be asking questions about why we were sneaking out of the house and checking people's rubbish at six in the morning. Basically it would mean being grounded for the rest of the summer and never having a sleep over again. The second option is that we could tell the police, but that would be worse than telling our parents. The third option is, we could kill the vampires."

"I'm not sure about any of those," interrupted Sean.

"Well that leaves option number four."

"Which is?" asked Sean.

"Which is, we just look after ourselves. We head in well before the sun sets, and at night we lock every window and stuff pillows up the chimney so that no bats can get in. Eventually the vampires will do something to draw the attention of the rest of the neighbourhood and then a grown-up, who knows more about these things, can deal with them."

Sean didn't say anything. I knew that this meant that this was his preferred option. He then placed the ball down on the penalty spot and took ten large strides backwards. Sean was rubbish at soccer. His penalty technique was to run as fast as he could toward the ball, before toe punting it as hard as possible towards the goal. Slowly, Sean began jogging, before picking up speed and pounding the ball with all his might. The ball shot through the air like a bullet from a gun. But instead of having to dive and make a save, I watched the ball fly high over the imaginary crossbar and into Miss Mangle's garden, where it landed in the middle of her beautiful border of flowers.

"Oh no," said Sean, "she'll kill me!"

Miss Mangle was scarier than any vampire! An elderly woman, she spent all day, every day, gazing out her window to see if anyone was doing something wrong, so she could pounce on them the minute that they did. In all honesty, Miss Mangle wasn't actually that old, but miserable people always look older than jolly people, and this lady was *so* miserable that she looked absolutely ancient. Picture the oldest, most crinkly person you know and imagine if someone had taken a photo of them, squashed it tightly into a ball and then unfolded it. That was Miss Mangle's face! But despite looking completely decrepit, she was like a cheetah if she was chasing after a misbehaving child.

Sean opened the creaky gate and tiptoed onto the lawn. The neighbourhood children were convinced that Miss Mangle let the gate get rusty on purpose, so that it would alert her to anyone entering her property. As Sean scanned the flower bed for the ball, I could see he was clenching his whole body tight, in expectation that the front door would open at any second and the wails of a screaming banshee would head his way. But nothing came. At last, Sean spotted his ball buried deep in amongst some tall yellow flowers and hurried to retrieve it. But as he reached in to gather the ball in his arms, he spotted something.

"Tom, get over here. Now!"

I raced over and looked down at what Sean was staring at. In front of us, underneath a laurel bush, lay Mr Tibbles, Miss Mangle's beloved cat. It lay motionless. Its marble-like eyes were wide open and a look of terror was frozen onto its face.

Sean darted toward a large oak tree at the edge of the garden.

"Where are you going?" I asked.

"I'm getting a poking stick. You know, to see if it's dead."

"Dead?" I said in disbelief. "Look at the poor thing. Of course it's dead!"

But Sean wasn't listening. He returned holding a long slender stick. "It's better to be safe than sorry," he said, jabbing sharply at the cat's torso.

As I continued to gaze at the poor creature that lay before me, I noticed something.

"Sean, look at this," I said.

Sean stopped poking the cat and squinted his eyes to focus at what I was pointing to - two small red circular marks on the Mr Tibble's neck, slightly camouflaged by its sleek black fur.

"Bite marks!" I exclaimed.

"You.....don't think," stammered Sean.

"Maybe?" I said. "What else would make those marks, if it wasn't a vampire?"

"I've never heard of a vampire killing a cat though. I thought it was just humans that they ate?" said Sean.

"I honestly don't know," I replied. "I had never really paid much attention to the lifestyle of vampires, until recently. For all we know they may drink all sorts of blood."

We then both stood quietly for a while, but I knew what we had to do next.

"I suppose we'd better go and tell Miss Mangle."

Sean began jumping around wildly, as if a swarm of bees had entered his trousers. "What? Why? She'll go bananas! Can't we just let her stumble across him the next time she comes out into the garden?"

"No, that's cruel. Besides, she may have seen something that can help explain what happened."

"Okay, but you're the one telling her," said Sean. "I did the last job."

"Hang on, I did." I stopped talking. What was the point? I just accepted that I was the one to do the job and began walking up the path toward the house. Heading up to Miss Mangle's residence was like a walk to the gallows. It was silly to be nervous of someone half your size and several times your age, yet, I was as nervous as a bald man wearing a wig on a wild and windy day.

When I reached the front door, it took every ounce of my courage to raise my hand and rap firmly on it. As I stood there, I rehearsed in my head what I was going to say. But as I continued to search for the right words, the door remained shut. I knocked again. Still, no response. After the third attempt, I turned around to Sean, who was cowering in the bushes behind me.

"She's not in," I said.

"What do you mean she's not in? She's always in."

Sean was right. Miss Mangle's daily routine was set in stone. She would leave the house at half past nine for a loaf of bread, a litre of milk and the Daily Mail, and upon her return she would head upstairs and spend the rest of the day sat staring out of her bedroom window, until she went to bed at a quarter to ten. It was the same every day, except on Sundays, when her son visited and took her out. The minute that she left the street, the residents of Sange Drive would all swarm out. Parents would be chit-chatting to each other, while the kids frolicked and galavanted. Huge games of rounders, hide and seek and tag would be played, and a seemingly endless supply of hot dogs and burgers would be sizzled and flipped on the lit barbeques. There was always a great buzz about the place, like a carnival. But the atmosphere would instantly vanish the minute her son's car rounded the corner to bring her home.

"Come to think of it, I actually haven't seen her for a few days." I said.

Sean's eyes gradually widened to the size of saucers. "They've killed her!" he said. "That's who Mark saw them burying in the garden. It wasn't the missing guy on the posters around town, or maybe it was both of them, but it was definitely Miss Mangle. They flew over here, drank Mr Tiddles' blood for starters and then they broke into the house and had Miss Mangle for the main course!"

"Hang on a minute, there must be a million reasons why she isn't here," I said, although I couldn't actually think of *one*.

"Okay, Sherlock. Like what?" Sean asked.

I thought for a while, and continued to draw a blank. This was admittedly getting stranger and stranger and I was finding it harder and harder to explain the events that were unfolding. I was now 99% sure that Sean was right. All signs pointed to the new neighbours at number 33 being vampires! But I needed to be 100% sure. "We'll have to investigate," I said. "Come on, let's go around the back and check the place for signs of a break in."

Nervously, we began jogging around the side of the property towards the rear of the house.

It was safe to say that no-one had ever ventured this deep into Miss Mangle's property before, as we rounded the corner and onto the back garden patio.

"Look in the windows and see if you can see anything," ordered Sean.

I pressed my face tightly to the glass, placing my hand above my eyes to shield my vision from the bright sunlight that hampered my view. As I studied Miss Mangle's living room I saw nothing suspicious. Everything looked pristine, and there was certainly no sign of a struggle. I scampered over to the adjacent kitchen window. Again, nothing. It was just as tidy as the living room. The counter tops were spotless. There wasn't even a crumb of toast to be seen. The crisp white cloth that covered the table was like untouched snow, while Miss Mangle's tartan shopping bag hung from the back of one of the chairs that were all tucked neatly underneath the table.

Miss Mangle's tartan shopping bag!

"Sean, get over here."

Sean darted over. I had a double take at him as he approached.

"What are you eating?" I asked.

"Just something I found in the garden," said Sean, as he finished chewing whatever it was that was in his mouth.

I didn't have time to question what on Earth Sean could have possibly found in the garden that was actually edible. This was more important. "Look, Miss Mangle's bag is on the back of the chair."

"Yeah, so what?" replied Sean.

I sighed. "Have you ever seen her leave her house without that bag?"

Sean thought for a second. "Actually, now you mention it, no I haven't."

"So, if she never leaves without it, and it is here, then that must mean one of two things - she is either in house somewhere, or she has gone somewhere without her bag, which she wouldn't do. Not unless it was serious!"

"Well if she's not in then you know where she's gone, don't you?" said Sean. "She's gone into the garden of number 33. Right, enough is enough. First the night time digging, then the bats, then the blood stained nightie that they put in the bin in the middle of the night and now Miss Mangle has gone missing. Do the maths - that's five strange things that have happened since your new neighbours moved in. I think we can safely say that they are *definitely* vampires!"

I had heard enough. I had been trying to keep an open mind, trying my best to explain all the crazy events logically, but Sean was right, for once. There had been so many odd things happen that I too was now utterly convinced that vampires were living at number 33. And this was simply unacceptable. "Right, we have no choice now but to sort this out ourselves. If they are killing people here, on Sange Drive, it could be any one of us next." And then, trying my best to sound brave, I said, "No vampires are going to hurt anyone else on *my* street!"

Vampire Hunters

It's amazing what you can find out on the internet. How anyone would know how to kill a vampire before Google was invented, I don't know. But it was now only a few taps of my Mum's phone screen and we were in possession of all of the facts.

"Sunlight kills them," I said, scrolling down the page, "but we knew that already. That's why they never leave the house during the day. And apparently vampires don't like garlic, but it doesn't say that it kills them. The other things that can destroy vampires are silver bullets, holy water and plunging a stake through their heart."

"How would you get a stake through their heart?" Sean asked. "That sounds a bit weird, if you ask me?"

No one was asking.

"Well, if the stake through the heart isn't a great option, then we only really have one choice, unless you know where we can get a gun and silver bullets?"

Sean shook his head.

"So the only real option we have is to kill them by soaking them with holy water. Now, here's the plan - we go down to St Barnaby's church and fill our water pistols with holy water. Once they're full, we'll come back and wait until the sun sets. Then we'll knock on the vampire's door and, when they open it, we'll spray them with the holy water. They'll die instantly and we'll be heroes."

"But what if they don't answer the door?" said Sean.

"Well, then at least we can keep the water pistols by our beds to protect ourselves at night time. It can't hurt."

"Sounds like a plan," said Sean. Then a smile popped up on his face. "Oh, Fat Jack's chip shop is on the way to the church. We should get something for lunch, seeing as we're passing anyway!"

Trip to St Barnaby's

I have to admit, we looked the business strutting up the hill that led to the church. Sean had slicked his hair back with water before leaving his house and I had my shades on. Both of us had our water guns resting on our shoulders. We were it. The real deal.

As we reached the courtyard of St Barnaby's, I thought what I always thought - that it would be a great setting for a horror film. The cold stone eyes of the creepy gargoyles that perched high on the drab grey walls seemed to always be watching, and it wouldn't be hard to imagine a zombie's hand poking up through the long dark grass that grew in irregular tufts around the sinister crooked gravestones. But yet, I always felt safe whenever I entered the church gates. I felt at peace. From the look on his face, I think the only thing Sean felt was indigestion from the huge portion of sausage and chips he had just wolfed down. But when we reached the thick oak doors of the church, a new emotion washed over the both of us - anxiety! For we could immediately see that there was a problem. Whether it had evaporated from the heat, or whether it had not been topped up for a while, I wasn't sure, but for whatever reason, the small stone font on the wall containing the holy water was nearly empty. There was barely enough water to fill a thimble, let alone the monstrous water guns we had brought with us. Sean had a squirter-blaster 3000. It could fire ten litres of water in five seconds. My gun was even stronger. It had super-charged ultra-rapid fire power! My Dad always joked that it was more like a pressure washer than a child's toy.

"Oh no, what are we going to do now?" fretted Sean, as we approached the font for a better look. "We won't be destroying any vampires with that tiny drop."

"Hang on," I said, "let's not get too worked up. It didn't say on the internet how much water you need to kill a vampire. Maybe a drop is enough? After all, a vampire is pure evil, so maybe just a small amount will be enough to destroy it?"

Sean didn't look convinced.

Suddenly I had an idea.

"I have an idea! We can take this small bit of water back to my house and mix it with some normal water. Enough to soak both of the vampires!"

"Hey, that's not a bad idea," Sean said. "But how are we going to get the water back to yours? Our water gun nozzles won't fit in the font."

Once more, my brain clicked into gear. The ideas were coming thick and fast now. "I know - we'll go to the corner shop and buy a packet of straws. I'll use one to suck up the water into my mouth, and then I'll spit the water back out through the straw and into my gun."

"Tombo, you're a genius," said Sean.

With that, we began the descent back down the hill towards the shop.

"We may as well get an ice cream while we're down there," said Sean.

Thy Holy Paddling Pool

"Right, it's full," I said, lifting the hose from the paddling pool that had been sat, unused, in my garden shed for the past three years.

"Shall I spray the holy water in then?" Sean asked.

"I suppose so," I replied.

Sean raised the gun to his shoulder and steadied himself. He closed one eye to aim, and…..ppfffffft. A measly dribble of water trickled out of the end of his water cannon.

"So, is *all* the water in the paddling pool holy now?" he asked.

"I'm not sure," I said. "I'm no expert. But hopefully when the small amount of holy

water we put in mixes with the normal water, it will all become holy?"

Sean furrowed his brow. "I'm not sure this is going to work. We should probably go back to the church tomorrow and try and get some more of the real stuff."

"No, we can't. Even if the font was full, I still doubt there would be enough to drench two vampires. Actually, I have just had a better idea. If we can find out how to turn water holy, then we can do it ourselves to the water in paddling pool, just to make sure."

So we opened the sliding door and went into the kitchen. Once again I made a grab for my Mum's phone, before typing in 'how to make holy water' into Google. I lowered my head into the screen to get a better look at what was involved.

"It says here that the first thing to do is to gather and bless some salt. Will you get some from the cupboard?"

But Sean didn't respond. He just stared off into space. I strongly suspected that the mention of salt had led him to think of hot chips and that he was now in a chip trance.

I decided to fetch it myself. I rummaged through the kitchen larder, moving out of the way numerous jars of out of date herbs and spices that my Mum had no intention of ever using, before I found it. I placed the shaker on the table and glanced down to the phone to read the words of psalm 103, which was needed to bless the salt and make it holy. It took a good while to read through the text, as although I was a fairly strong reader, many of the words weren't those you would use every day. Flourisheth, redeemeth, dominion, iniquities! All words that I could just about read, but ones that I had to take extra care with. After all, I didn't know if saying one incorrectly would affect the holiness of the water.

So far so good.

But I sighed after reading step three. "Shoot, it says here that you should use pure water. It is supposed to be water from a spring, not water from a tap. But it's too late, we've already filled the paddling pool."

Sean smiled and shook his head. "The paddling pool water isn't from a tap," he snorted. "It's from a hose, you doughnut!"

"But the hose…" I stopped, and carried on. There was little to do about it now. I just needed to continue and hope for the best. I sprinkled the salt into the paddling pool and spoke the final blessing needed to conclude the ritual. "May this salt and water be mixed together in the name of the Father, and of the Son, and of the Holy Spirit," I made the sign of the cross, "Amen."

As I rose my head, I was greeted by the image of Sean repeatedly raising his waving arms up high in the sky and then down to his knees, like an Indian Shaman.

"What on Earth are you doing?" I asked. "You look like the world's worst aerobics instructor."

"What? I just got caught up in the moment is all," said Sean. "So is that it? Is all the water definitely holy now?"

"I don't know," I replied. "But it's as holy as it's ever going to get. I suppose we will find out for sure later, when we spray it on the vampires."

Sean puffed out his cheeks in an exaggerated fashion. "This just got really real. Right, we need to plan this very carefully."

The Soaking!

The plan had taken around seventeen seconds to come up with. The rest of the day had dragged out longer. Especially the last hour. I guess it's true what they say about a watched kettle never boiling because the last ten minutes, where we had sat and watched the rim of the late evening sun shrink ever smaller as it slipped slowly down over the horizon, felt like a decade. But then, finally, it did happen. It vanished. The sun had set!

We stood on the pavement of the street, looking at the neighbours' gloomy house that loomed large in front of us, and I knew that it was time to put the plan into action.

"Okay, let's do this!" I said. I was trying my best to be brave. One of us had to be, because I had noticed that Sean was unusually quiet and that he had begun shaking. Shaking like the bucketful of jelly he had noisily slurped down for his dessert.

"Don't worry," I said, even though *I* was worried. Very, very worried. "There's nothing to be scared about." Another lie. This was probably the single most-scary thing that any eleven year old had ever done. Ever!

"Okay," said Sean. "Let's be quick though. In and out!"

That sounded good to me.

We looked at each other. Nothing was said, but a million words were spoken in that glance.

Then we began walking toward their house. My feet felt heavy. It felt like I was walking across a beach of wet sand in a full suit of armour. But, by putting one foot in front of the other, we eventually reached the short concrete path that cut across their lawn to the front door. Slowly, we walked up it.

Sean was shaking even more now. It wasn't the gentle wobble of a jelly on a plate any more. It was now more like the convulsion of a jelly that had been placed on top of an old tumble drier on full pelt.

And at that moment I knew that it was all down to me, so I lifted the knocker and rapped loudly three times. Instantly we got into position, raising our loaded guns and aiming them squarely at the door. And there we waited, ready.

But nothing.

"There's no-one answering," said Sean, stating the obvious. "Maybe they're still asleep in their coffins or something?"

I was deeply frustrated. We had come so far that I really didn't want to leave without sorting the problem out, so I plucked up the courage to kneel down to the letterbox. I carefully pushed in the flap and placed my eye to the slit in the door. At once, I recoiled.

"There's a girl there!" I panicked. "She's standing in the hallway!"

Sean started leaping about like a dog who had just seen its master grab its lead, ready for walkies. "Right, right, what will we do? What will we do?" he stammered and spluttered.

I knew what we had to do! You hear about people in dangerous situations who do amazingly courageous things without even thinking about it. People who dash into burning buildings to save their loved ones. People who somehow summon superhuman strength to lift cars when someone is trapped underneath. I now knew how they felt. I knelt down and lodged the barrel of my gun firmly into the letterbox.

"Take that, you bloodsucking scum!" I roared. Adrenaline had overtaken my fear. I was in the zone. I began pumping the barrel of the gun back and forth, spraying large volumes of

water into the neighbours' hallway. And in no time at all, my gun was empty.

"Quick, give me yours," I said, holding out my hand to receive Sean's gun. Then I sprayed more and more water into the house. As the last drips of water drained from Sean's water pistol, I yanked the end from the letterbox. "Let's get out of here," I said. And then we ran. We ran as fast as we could, back down the path and out of Sange Drive towards Sean's house, a few streets away.

Clearing the Air

The light in Sean's treehouse had escaped quickly since we had clambered up. The leafy canopy meant that it was never that bright anyway, even in the middle of the day, but it was now getting downright dark. We had been up here for about half an hour, totally unsure of what to do next. Did the water drench the vampire standing in the hallway? Was the water holy enough? Was there enough of it to destroy the vampire? There was no way of knowing really, so we just sat, nestled in the large beech tree, half discussing our next move and half too afraid to come down. We would be forced to climb down soon though, as it was drawing ever closer to nine o'clock - the time we needed to be home. Usually we would push our luck and stay out until ten past - quarter past on some days - but with the all vampire stuff that had been happening I was in the mind to head home early, something unheard of in those carefree days before the new neighbours arrived. Days that now seemed nothing more than a fond and distant memory. I looked again at my watch and tried my best to make out the time, when all of a sudden something made me jump out of my anxious skin.

"Tom, Sean, get down here now!" shouted Sean's Mum from the garden beneath us.

"And hurry up!"

We both looked at each other.

"She sounds mad," I said. "What's all this about?

Sean shrugged his shoulders and made a strange face, which I took as meaning that he didn't know. We scurried over to the entrance of the treehouse and carefully descended the ladder into the garden. The crickets were in full voice, as we strode across the garden and through the back door of Sean's house.

"In the living room!" came Sean's Mum's short voice.

As we entered the living room, I saw Sean's Mum frowning. And this was some frown. Deep black lines crackled across her forehead like forked lightening, which suggested big trouble. My Mum standing there with her arms folded tightly, confirmed it. Our Mums were clearly simmering with anger, and perhaps ready to boil over!

Usually this sight would have worried me greatly, but today I barely registered them, because all of my attention was on the two people I had noticed sitting on the sofa. Well, people is one way to describe them. They actually looked more like giant praying mantises than human beings. One was a man in his early fifties, and the other a girl in her late teens. Both were very tall and gangly with deathly pale skin and hair as white as freshly fallen snow. While the girl had her head bobbed, the man looked intently at us with wide eyes that bubbled a volcanic red.

"Tom, Sean, this is the Orloks. They're the new neighbours from number 33. Now, would you care to explain to them, and to us, why you sprayed their hallway with water earlier?" demanded Sean's Mum.

Me and Sean stood like statues, first looking at each other, then at the Orloks, then at Sean's

Mum and then at mine, before finally looking back at each other.

Finally, Sean blurted out, "They're vampires! They don't go out in the daylight, they turn into bats, they've killed Mr Tibbles and Miss Mangle and then they buried her in the garden and put her bloody robes into the bin.

And just look at them sat there, all weird with their red eyes. They're evil. Now don't come any closer you monsters, or I'll spray you with holy water."

Mr Orlok sat for a while, staring at Sean, before a crease started folding across his face. A smile emerged. It gradually increased in size until it got so big that it burst open with a snigger, which soon turned into a full blown chortle. Through his hearty laugh, he managed to mutter, "Vampires. Oh dear, that is too much."

"You're denying it then, are you?" said Sean. "Well, if you're not vampires then why not eat some garlic bread?" With that, Sean sunk his hand into the pocket of his shorts and fished out a hunk of baguette, smothered in garlic butter.

"You keep garlic bread in your pocket to protect yourself from vampires?" my Mum snorted.

Sean looked at her for a moment in confusion, before shaking his head, "No. I always carry around garlic bread in my pocket - in case I get peckish between meals."

This brought even more howls of laugher from Mr Orlok.

I decided it was time to speak up. "So if you aren't vampires, then how do you explain all the strange things that have happened since you moved in?"

"Well," began Mr Orlok, who had finally caught his breath, "the reason we do not leave the house during the day is because we are albinos, which I'm sure you can see for yourselves."

Sean scoffed, "Yeah, right. If you were albinos then you would be living in an igloo in the North Pole, not on Sange Drive."

The teenage girl, who had sat completely silent and motionless until now, slowly raised her head. "That's Eskimos, you idiot," she uttered in a monotone voice, before lowering her head again and returning to her default position.

Mr Orlok nodded in agreement. "Albinism is a condition where the people affected do not have pigmentation in their skin, hair and eyes. This is why we appear very pale and why our hair is white and our eyes pink. And with this condition we cannot go out in strong sunlight. Having no pigment in our skin means that if we did, we would get sunburned in a very short space of time. And, as I'm sure you have noticed, it's been a *very* hot August. It's the reason we moved in during the night and the reason we are not seen in the day. We often sleep in the afternoon when it is at its hottest and then rise in the evening, when it has cooled down. It's quite a common practice in warmer countries. A siesta, they call it."

"Well, what about all the other stuff," I asked.

"The 'bloody' robes you found when you were rooting through our rubbish were Cordelia's.

She had been painting her bedroom red. Simply redecorating is all. The bats are something we seemed to inherit. It's an old house and once we moved in we discovered that we have a few of the furry critters living in the attic. We have pest control coming next week to sort it. The cat - well the cat we are to blame for. And for that we are deeply sorry."

I looked at Sean. This was it. They were going to admit it.

"During the chaos of the move and unpacking all of our belongings, Cordelia's pet python escaped. When we eventually tracked it down, we found it had bitten and killed the neighbour's pet cat. We went to the house to explain and apologise, but when we did, the lady took a funny turn - a suspected heart attack! Of course, we rushed her to hospital and she's been there ever since."

"Sorry to interrupt you, Mr Orlok," said Sean's Mum, "thanks for explaining, but there is really no need. All of this is utterly ridiculous!"

"It's not ridiculous," said Sean. "Okay, so they may not be vampires, but they're definitely murderers. You never explained why your back garden is dug up. We know you buried that guy in there. The one that went missing at *exactly* the same time that you moved in!"

Mr Orlok looked at us in confusion. "My back garden isn't dug up?"

And that's when another swell of laughter filled the room. But this time it wasn't from Mr Orlok. It came from the top of the stairs.

It was strange to hear Mark laugh. I hadn't heard him do so since he turned goth, or emo. I think he found it strange himself. His robotic-bursts-of-laughter sounded as if he was trying to remember how it was done.

"You two are *so* gullible," he said, plodding down the stairs. "That dug up patch was just a small bit of grass that me and Draven dug up in the park. We took a photo of it to wind you up. I cannot believe you fell for it."

"Mark! That's not funny, or very nice," said Sean's Mum.

"I'm sorry, Mum," said Mark, wiping his eyes and smearing wet mascara all over his face while doing so, "I was only messing with them. I would never have done it if I knew they would go and do something like this." He turned to the Orloks. "And I would like to apologise to you, Mr Orlok. And also to you, Cordelia." And as he looked at her and said her name, his face went bright red for some reason?

My Mum unfolded her tightly knotted arms. "I'm so sorry that my son and his friend have done this to you, and I'm sure they would like to apologise - *wouldn't you boys!"*

We looked at each other sheepishly.

"Sorry," we said, trying our best to sound like we meant it.

"Now the boys will pay for any damages, of course. Did anything break or get destroyed when they sprayed the water into your house?"

"No, no, not at all. I don't want your money. I just wanted to clear the air. I don't want the poor boys to worry. Mind you, if we could ask a favour?" said Mr Orlok, glancing over to his daughter. "If you ever require a babysitter then perhaps you could bear Cordelia in mind. She is starting university next month and is saving up. The extra money would be a great help to her."

My Mum smiled. "Isn't that a co-incidence? Our last babysitter was the daughter of the previous owners of number 33 and we've been looking for someone ever since. You know what - my husband and I haven't been out for ages. Why doesn't Cordelia come over tomorrow night to mind Tom?" She turned to Sean's Mum. "Why don't you and Tony come as well, Susan? Mark can mind Sean. It's the least he could do. I'll ring and book a table somewhere as soon as I get home."

Then our Mums did this thing that only mums do - they seemed to turn into pigeons before our very eyes and began flapping their hands in excitement and cooing.

Mr Orlok seemed happy too.

"Oh, that's wonderful, isn't it Cordelia?" he said excitedly.

"Yes, that's fantastic," mumbled Cordelia from under her mop of long white hair.

"Did she just say, *fang*tastic?" asked Sean.

"No! She said fantastic," replied Sean's Mum, through gritted teeth.

My Mum quickly changed the subject. "So we'll see you tomorrow then, Cordelia. And once again, I'm very sorry about all this. I hope we can put all this behind us and become great friends."

Sean's Mum nodded in agreement. "Yes, it was wonderful to finally meet you."

"Yes, you too," said Mr Orlok, as he and Cordelia stood up and sloped awkwardly out of the room.

Sean's Mum followed the Orloks to the door and waved at them politely as she closed it behind them. But the very second the door shut, our Mums flung around sharply and glowered at us, while we stood feeling small in the middle of the room.

"Vampires! What on Earth were you thinking? Ridiculous! The sooner you two get back to school the better," said my Mum.

Sean's Mum was in total agreement. "That poor family. They must have got an awful fright. Now Sean, I hope this is the end of all this vampire nonsense!"

Cordelia's Babysitting Service

I sat on the end of my bed and listened to the conversation from downstairs.

"So where are you going to eat?" asked Cordelia, politely.

"Lanzini's," replied my Mum, putting on her snootiest voice. "Oh, it's lovely there. And ever-so-posh. You can tell it's a really fancy place as the portions are absolutely tiny. You're still starving when you finish, so we'll probably go to McDonald's and get a drive through on the way home. But we won't be too late. Thanks again for minding Tom. Help yourself to anything you want from the fridge, and you have my number, if you need it."

Then I heard the front door close and my Mum plod down the gravel driveway to the car that was revving wildly - Dad was clearly keen to get to his meal. I listened to the car crackle out of the driveway and the engine grow fainter as it sped down the road. The very second that the noise of the car evaporated into the atmosphere, another noise took its place - it was my walkie-talkie crackling, before a distorted voice shuddered through the battered old speaker.

"So they've gone and left you then?" said Sean. "It's just you and the vampire now, so keep your wits about you, whatever you do."

Using my thumb, I pressed down the button on the side of the walkie-talkie. "She's not a vampire. That was all cleared up yesterday. It's time you let it go. Anyway, how do you know my Mum and Dad have left?"

"I'm watching your house," said Sean. "I told you, I'm not convinced by all that mumbo jumbo that those vampires were spouting yesterday, so I'll be keeping a close eye on your place all evening, just in case you need me. Also, when I was over earlier, I prepared a few things to help you protect yourself. There is a piece of garlic bread in the fridge, your water pistol is loaded with holy water in the bathroom and there is a stake under your bed. I didn't tell you until now as I didn't want you to freak out. You'll need to keep a cool head if you want to stay alive."

"Um...thanks," I replied, "but really, you shouldn't have bothered. What I'm more concerned about is how awkward this all is. I've got a babysitter downstairs who I sprayed water at yesterday because I thought she was a vampire. It's so embarrassing. I suppose I should just go down and face her. If I apologise again, maybe she'll let me come out for a kick around before bed? Okay, I better go. We'll chat later. Over and out."

I threw the walkie-talkie to the floor. I hated that thing. Talking to Sean would be so much easier if I had a phone, but Mum and Dad were technophobes so they always said, no way. Phones rot your brain, they said. Turns kids into zombies. Of course they both had the latest phones, but that was because they needed them for work. I was forbidden to even ask the question until I was thirteen. And even then I knew what the answer would be.

I took a deep breath, to help pluck up the courage to head down the stairs. When I reached the bottom few steps, I could see the back of Cordelia's head. She was sat on the sofa watching a programme on our huge, ultra HD T.V that Dad had bought in the January sales.

"Hi Cordelia, how are you?" I said, my voice all croaky. "Listen, I'm sorry again about yesterday. I feel terrible about the whole thing." I paused for a moment, before chancing my arm. "Um, would it be alright if I went to out to play for a small while before bedtime?"

Cordelia shot around like a whippet. She looked directly at me with a red-hot intensity in her eyes. "No! You are to go upstairs and go to bed," she snapped.

"But it's only eight o'clock. I don't go to bed until ten during the summer holidays," I said. "And I'm allowed to stay out until nine."

Cordelia didn't move a muscle. She continued to glare at me with those burning red eyes. Eyes that stared so hard that I felt I may just burst into flames at any second! Suddenly, Cordelia threw her arm out and pointed to the top of the stairs. "Bed. Now!" she barked.

I couldn't argue. Not after yesterday. And to be honest, even though I now knew that she

wasn't a vampire, I was still a little bit terrified of her, too. So I turned and trudged back up the stairs, a little confused by what had just happened. Was Cordelia still mad about the water spraying incident? Or was she just a super strict babysitter? Either way, the end result was the same - I was heading up to bed.

Upon entering my bedroom, I picked up my walkie-talkie from the floor, before flinging myself back onto my mattress.

"Sean, are you there? Over."

"Tom, are you okay? Are you still alive?" replied Sean.

"Of course I am! The very fact I'm talking to you now suggests that I am still alive, doesn't it?" I said.

"Alright, grumpy, don't get your knickers in a twist. So what's up then?"

"I just spoke with Cordelia. She was super harsh. She ordered me to go to bed. It's only eight o'clock. What am I going to do?" I sighed as I looked around my sparse room. The T.V was downstairs. The PlayStation was, too. All that there was to do was to play with some old toys that I had grown out of years ago but hadn't had the heart to throw away, just in case they came alive when I went to sleep, like in Toy Story.

"You could just sneak out," suggested Sean.

"No, I can't," I said miserably. "I can't get into any more trouble after yesterday. I may just go to bed. If I manage to get to sleep early then at least I can wake up early and make the most of tomorrow."

"No, don't do that!" said Sean. "That's exactly what she wants you to do. The minute you're asleep, you're done for. She'll bite your neck and you'll be dead and buried in their garden, like the others!"

"She – is – not – a - vampire," I said, pausing between every word to hammer the point home. "Now, I am going to bed, but if it will put your mind at rest, I doubt I'll be able to sleep anyway. It's way too early. Over, and out."

"It's your funeral," said Sean. "But I don't care what you say, I still think she *is* a vampire, so I won't be going anywhere. I'll be here watching and waiting for her to make her move. I won't let anything happen to you. Over and out...for now."

Slowly, I put on my pyjamas. Then I drew the curtains and clambered into bed. Despite my curtains being thick and the sun having set, the room was still fairly well lit. I'll never get to sleep, I thought. It's too early. It's too bright. I'm not tired. I could be lying here for hours. This is complete waste of.

Little Miss Invisible

"Tom, are you there?"

Raising my heavy arm from the bed, I fumbled around on the chest of drawers for my walkie-talkie. What time was it? How long had it been since I nodded off?

"Yeah, I'm here. What's up?"

"You need to get out of there," said Sean. "I was right - she is a vampire!"

Immediately, I shot bolt upright in bed. All the tiredness shot out of my body, like a bomb had just exploded inside me. "What are you on about? If you're joking, then it isn't funny."

"It's not a joke," said Sean.

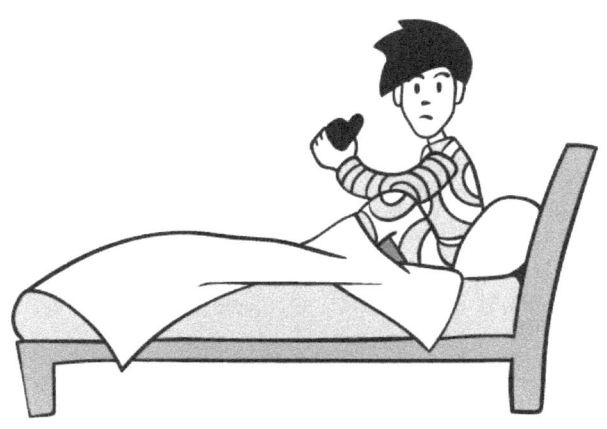

I could hear panic in his voice. If it was a wind up, then he was doing a very good job of it.

"I was doing my perimeter check of your house, to see if everything was okay, and when I walked past the living room window I saw that the T.V remote was floating through the air in the middle of the room."

I instantly relaxed. "Ah, come on now," I said, smiling to myself, "now I know that you're joking."

But Sean wasn't letting up. "No, honestly! I saw the remote floating through the air. And that's when I realised something - I was looking into your living room mirror! When I got closer to the window, I saw that Cordelia was holding the remote, changing channels. Don't you see? She was there, but I couldn't see her in the mirror. She had no reflection. Vampires have no reflection!"

I sat completely numb on the bed. I felt sick. Sean wasn't one for cruel practical jokes, but this couldn't really be happening, could it?

"Tom, just get out of there. But be careful, if she sees you, you'll be in serious trouble."

Leaping from my bed, I began to pace in small circles around the room. I was in a state of panic. I couldn't think. My head was full of clouds. And not those wispy summertime ones that look like tissue paper. It was big black thunderclouds that filled every inch of my head. I was completely lost. I didn't know what to do? But then I remembered that Sean had left me some items I could use to protect myself. It would be some small comfort knowing that I was armed, while I found a safe escape route. I couldn't get to the piece of garlic bread in the fridge, but I did have the stake under my bed and the water pistol in the bathroom. But which would be better? The stake was right here, but killing Cordelia with a stake would mean getting very up close and personal. Too close for my liking. I could fire the water pistol from distance, but getting that would involve leaving my room. And I wasn't sure the water pistol would even work anyway. There was no way of knowing if the water I had sprayed at Cordelia yesterday had even touched her? If it had, then it clearly wasn't holy enough!

My thoughts went to and fro, back and forth, like a ping pong ball being smacked around in a table tennis rally. My decision - I would take both. The water pistol was my preferred option, but if it didn't work then at least I would have the stake to use as a back-up.

"Sean, I'm going to grab the stake, and then get the water pistol, and then I'll try and escape," I said. "Don't contact me again until I contact you. I don't want Cordelia to hear me. Over and out!"

"Be careful, mate," said Sean. "Right, I'm going to move your trampoline underneath your bathroom window. So once you have the water pistol you can jump down and we can get out of here. Over and out."

I didn't like the sound of Sean's plan. But that was a worry for later. First I needed to arm myself. Being very careful not to make a sound, I lay down on the floor and reached my arm under my bed to fetch the stake. But as I fumbled around blindly, I couldn't find any trace of a sharp wooden object that I could plunge through Cordelia's dark heart. Eventually my hand did stumble across something, but it wasn't the pointed wooden object I had anticipated finding. Instead, I found myself gripping a soft, warm lump of squidgy flesh, and I knew instantly that Sean had got a beef steak, instead of a wooden stake.

My only hope was the water pistol. I hopped back onto my feet and moved quickly and quietly over to the bedroom door. But as I placed my hand on the doorknob, something made me stop quite still. Somebody was coming up the stairs!

Bad Babysitter

The dark clouds were back. But now they had burst and it was raining cats and dogs inside my head. Any thoughts on how to escape were being washed away before they could form. I was in a frenzy. I didn't know what to do. I could hide under the bed, but then Cordelia would surely find me. I could jump out the window, but I was afraid of heights and it was a fair drop. Telling Sean to put the trampoline under my bedroom window instead of the bathroom would help reduce the fall, and the impact, but it would take him too long. The trampoline was only a metre or so from the bathroom window, positioning it underneath my bedroom window would involve dragging it the whole way across the back lawn. And it was very heavy. There was only one thing that I could think of to do. It was a terrible option really, but I had nothing else. So I reached back under the bed and grabbed the steak, before jumping into bed and pulling the covers tightly over me, to pretend to be asleep. Maybe Sean had got this all wrong? Maybe he was joking? Maybe Cordelia was just coming to check on me, like all good babysitters do? Maybe?

I lay as stiff as a board, as the handle of the door slowly turned and a thin slither of light from the landing cut into the dimness of my room like a dagger. My hearing seemed super-sensitive and I could hear every one of Cordelia's gentle footsteps padding across my floor. And then everything fell silent for what seemed like forever.

"Are you awake?" came a whispered voice.

I remained frozen.

"Are you awake, boy?" Cordelia repeated.

I continued to lay completely still, my eyes squeezed shut.

"I don't mind if you are asleep," said Cordelia. "It would be easier if you were, but in fact, I'd actually prefer it if you were awake."

My head was spinning. My heart was beating out of my chest and bucketfuls of cold sweat began pouring out of me, like I was an oversaturated sponge being rung out. I hoped beyond hope that this was some weird dream, some sick joke….something. Anything! Anything other than what it appeared to be!

"Dad doesn't normally approve of this. He always says that we are never to hunt too near to home. It's one of the golden rules we follow. But for you, he is allowing me to make an exception. You see we were planning to move tomorrow anyway. We never stay anywhere more than a month. But this time we are moving sooner than expected. This neighbourhood has been nothing but trouble. The nights have been so short that it hasn't been easy to hunt. I would never normally resort to eating a cat, but I was *so* hungry. And then, when that stupid old hag spotted me in the act, I had to deal with her right in the middle of the street, which isn't our normal style. And then you two pesky kids started poking your noses into our business, drawing attention to us and causing us grief. You know, you only just missed me with that holy water yesterday. Lucky for me, unlucky for you! Anyway, it's all worked out fine in the end. I get to drink your blood now, and then my Dad will kill your little friend later, and then we will be on our way. Oh, I've been so looking forward to eating you. I've thought of nothing else since we met yesterday. There is nothing more delicious than young blood - especially when it is O positive. Now boy, you may wonder why I'm telling you all this? Well, it's because I'm hoping that you are awake and that with my every word your heart is beating faster and faster, because a racing heart makes blood taste all the sweeter!"

With that, Cordelia leapt up onto the foot of my bed. So soft and graceful was her landing, that I barely felt it. It was more like a dragonfly landing on a calm pool of water than a large teenage girl bounding onto my mattress.

"Right, enough talking," snarled Cordelia. "It's dinnertime!"

Instantly I flipped over onto my back, at the same very moment that Cordelia pounced on top of me.

"Oh goody, you are awake!" she snarled. Her eyes were on fire. It was like looking down into the heart of two soon-to-erupt red hot volcanoes. And then I noticed her fangs. Fangs that seemed to be growing longer before my very eyes! And now Cordelia looked more like a wild animal than a young lady.

I held out my outstretched arms and pushed her back with all my might, as she began gnashing ferociously at my slender neck.

"It's useless to resist," she hissed, thick strands of saliva dripping from her fangs and onto my face. "I'm going to kill you. You do know that, right?"

Inching ever closer to my neck, I knew that I couldn't hold her off for much longer. I tried to push her off but she was too strong. But I had to do something!

Cordelia was creeping ever nearer, snapping frantically at my plump, ripe neck like an excited crocodile.

So I summoned every ounce of my strength, and with all my might, I swung the sirloin steak up from under the duvet and it clattered into Cordelia's face with a loud meaty thud. Now, while it didn't destroy Cordelia, as a wooden stake may have, it did have the effect of unbalancing her just enough to allow me to sharply roll out from under her.

I fell off the bed and onto the floor with a bang.

I knew that this was my chance - perhaps my only chance - to escape. I sprang to my feet, grabbed my walkie-talkie from the chest of drawers and ran out of the door, slamming it shut behind me. I darted into the bathroom and slammed that door too, before putting down the latch to lock it. As I scanned the room for my water pistol, I heard a pounding at the door.

"There's no escape, boy!" Cordelia sneered. "You're locked in and there's no way out. And if you're looking for your water gun full of holy water then you're out of luck. I emptied it earlier. So you may as well just come out now. I'll make it quick and painless for you, if you make it easy for me."

I could hardly breathe.

Cordelia had now begun charging at the door at full pelt, smashing into it with such force that the wooden frame was shaking at the hinges. It surely wouldn't be long until she broke through!

A Friend in Need is a Friend Indeed

I felt like a fly stuck in a web. I continued to watch the door shudder and shake, as Cordelia threw herself against it with all her might. I knew I was running out time. I had but one hope.

"Sean, Sean, come in, Sean!"

Instantly, the walkie-talkie crackled back. "Tom, are you okay?"

"You were right," I said. "The Orloks are vampires. And Cordelia's trying to kill me! I'm locked in the bathroom and she emptied my water pistol. I'm trapped and there's no way out!"

The reply was instant.

"Don't worry, Tom. Just look out into the garden."

I ran over to the edge of the room and looked out of the window. I could see Sean frantically waving at me from the grass beneath me. He had moved the trampoline right under the window and he gave a smile and a thumbs up when I caught his eye.

"You can jump down onto the trampoline to escape."

I looked down, and immediately I felt like puking. I had a phobia of heights. It had been that way since I was seven and we had gone on a school trip to the local adventure playground, where I climbed to the top of the space dive, which all the local residents ominously referred to as, the death slide, but had been too afraid to go down. Eventually I had hurtled down the near vertical slide, but only after Billy Maddox had pushed me over the edge, giving me the fright of my life and two red raw friction burns on each of my tender knees to boot.

I peered down at the trampoline beneath me. It probably wasn't that big of a drop, but to me, from where I was standing, it felt like I was about to jump out of an aeroplane without a parachute, while attempting to land on postage stamp.

"Come on, you'll be fine," urged Sean, waving his hands at me, to beckon me down.

I looked back at the door. Cordelia wasn't giving up. I could see the wood beginning to splinter and split. Fine hairline cracks were developing into deep, thick grooves, and I knew that it would be only minutes until Cordelia broke through. And then that would be that! It would be like a lion being let loose in the gazelle pen at the zoo. I knew I had no choice but to jump. Very carefully, I leaned out the window. But I couldn't do it.

"I...I can't do it," I whimpered.

"Right then, plan B," said Sean. "I have my water pistol here and I just filled it up from the paddling pool. I'll throw it up to you through the window and you can spray Cordelia when she gets in."

"But what if it doesn't reach," I said. "Or what if I don't catch it?"

"Well, we don't have much choice, do we? Look, there really are only two choices - jump, or spray!"

Sean was right. The door was now hanging from one of its hinges. Cordelia was nearly in!

"Okay, throw it up," I said.

Hopping onto the trampoline, Sean began bouncing higher and higher and higher, to get as close to the window as possible. "You'll have to reach out to catch it," he said.

I leaned out of the window, as much as I could manage, and held open my trembling hands. Once I was in position, Sean jumped, and when he reached his highest point, he threw the water pistol into the air. It spun and span and spinned as it hurtled toward me.

When it got near, I quickly clasped my hands together and managed to catch the faintest hold of the barrel of the gun. Manoeuvring my hands to get a better grip, I then lifted the gun in through the window.

Suddenly, the bathroom door burst open.

Cordelia staggered into the room.

"Nowhere to run now, boy!" she snarled.

At once, I turned to face Cordelia. I raised the gun and squeezed the trigger hard. A huge jet of water flew through the air, soaking her from head to toe.

"Arrgh, it's burning!" Cordelia yelled, as she tore at her face and clothes in a feeble attempt to remove the water she had just been doused in. I continued to spray Cordelia, who wailed the most horrific of screams and whirled around manically. Her wild jerking

movements reminded me of the midnight disco dancing my Uncle Dave did at all the family weddings. Cordelia continued cavorting and contorting, like a broken robot, before she suddenly darted toward me. As she approached, I continued to spray her with the last dregs of water in the gun, before jumping sharply out of the way, leaving Cordelia hurtling towards, and out of, the open window. I rushed over to watch her plummet to the ground. She fell, bang smack, into the middle of the paddling pool, spraying the water out in all directions.

Cordelia writhed around in the empty paddling pool for a few seconds, before she suddenly went very silent and very still. And now, Cordelia didn't look like Cordelia any more. Her skin was all black and smouldering and had crinkled up, like an overly toasted marshmallow.

"I think she's dead," Sean called up to me. I then watched him pace around the garden and I knew that he was searching for a poking stick.

Meanwhile, I stood in shock at the window, trying to catch my breath in the fresh air. But then, something caught my eye - the upstairs light in the Orlok's house switched on!

One Down, One to Go

I hurtled down the stairs, through the hall and the kitchen, before bursting into the back garden.

"I just saw the light go on in the Orlok's house," I said to Sean. "Mr Orlok is at home. He probably heard Cordelia screaming. What will we do?"

"Relax, we'll just spray him with some holy water, too," said Sean, calmly.

But when we looked into the paddling pool, we saw that the holy water was gone. Cordelia's fall had caused the entire contents to spray out onto the thankful grass. A small trickle remained at the bottom but it was not nearly enough to fill even a fraction of a water pistol's tank.

"Okay, new plan," said Sean. "We'll go to my house and ring the police."

"I'm not sure about that," I said. "We'll be sitting ducks there, and we don't want to put Mark in danger as well. Plus, how long will it take for the police to arrive? That's if they even believe us and come at all!"

"Well we haven't really got much choice," said Sean. "With no holy water, the only other way we could kill Mr Orlok is by exposing him to sunlight, and we won't have any of that for hours!" Suddenly, a lightbulb went on in Sean's mind. "Hang on, what about the stake that I put under your bed?" he suggested.

"No, I don't think that will work," I said.

As we pondered our next move, an eerie fluttering noise began to fill the air. The strange noise grew ever louder. And that's when I saw it - a bat flying through the sky! It flapped around in the air for a while, before descending into the garden, where it landed, in a puff of bright purple smoke, on the ground. When the smoke cleared, a tall figure stood menacingly in front of us. It was Mr Orlok, who looked in horror at the scene before him.

"My dear sweet Cordelia. What have you boys done?" he wailed.

Mr Orlok knelt down to the sticky black ooze that used to be his daughter and gently lifted her blob of a head. "My daughter. My

beautiful daughter. Why? WHY? She never hurt a fly."

At which point, Sean turned to me and whispered in my ear, "Well that's a whopping great lie, isn't it?"

Mr Orlok buried his head into his daughter and began to sob uncontrollably.

While Mr Orlok was consumed by grief, I sensed it was the perfect time to escape, so I elbowed Sean and mouthed to him, "Come on let's go."

I began to tiptoe quietly past the grieving vampire. Sean trailed close behind. As we made our way past Mr Orlok, Sean bent down to pick up a swing ball racket that lay on the grass.

"For protection," he whispered.

Gradually, inch by inch, we crept ever closer to our exit, when all of a sudden, Mr Orlok raised his head. His eyes burned bright crimson and he snarled at us, displaying a long pair of razor sharp fangs!

"You'll pay for this!" he growled, as he leapt to his feet.

"Quick, run!" I shouted.

We began sprinting as fast as our legs would carry us, down the path toward the front of the house. As we passed, I grabbed hold of the handle of my bike that was propped up against the wall at the side of the house and jumped on.

"Get on!" I ordered.

Sean hopped on the back of the bike and wrapped one arm tightly around my waist, while still keeping a firm hold of the racket with the other. I then began pedalling furiously out of the driveway. As we bombed down the street, Sean glanced back.

"Faster, Tom!" he shouted. "Mr Orlok is running after us. And he's fast!"

The back of my legs were already burning. My thigh muscles felt like they were being stretched to breaking point, like a taught elastic band about to snap apart at any minute, but I dug deep to find the energy needed to push that bit harder. After all, this was life or death! Luckily, Sange Drive was situated on the top of a small hill, which meant that when we reached the end of the road the pedalling became a bit easier. It also meant that we were picking up speed by the second. It was gradual, at first, but then we got faster and faster and faster, until my legs weren't doing the work anymore. They just sat on the pedals as they spun around and around with a mind of their own.

"Keep going, we're losing him," said Sean, continuing to glance back.

When we reached the bottom of the hill, Sean once again peeked over his shoulder.

"He's gone," he cheered in delight. But no sooner had he uttered these words, when all of a sudden, a small black object shot over our heads.

"Oh no, he's back. And he's turned into a bat!" said Sean.

I too now afforded a peek behind me. In the night sky, I could see two dots of fiery red, like two tiny candles flickering in the darkness. The red pin pricks grew to small circles as the bat drew near. And then it began diving toward us at speed. I had to duck and weave out of the way to avoid being hit, and as I did so, the wheels of the bike began to wobble and buckle.

"He's trying to knock us off," I yelled. "Do something!"

"Just keep us steady," Sean ordered, planting his feet on the rear mudguard and raising himself up on the back of the bike. With great purpose and authority, Sean raised the racket in his hand and stated, "Don't worry, I'll sort him out. I'm not Sange Drive swing ball champion for the last three years running for nothing!"

Sean took great pride in the fact he was the street champion, even though the 'tournament' consisted only of himself, a less-than-interested me, and my Mum - and she didn't even use her strong hand!

Sean balanced himself, while keeping a firm focus on the red eyes of the bat that once more flew towards us. And then, once the bat was in range, he swung that racket as hard as he could.

Boof!

The very centre of the racket smashed into the bat, which sent it reeling back from where it came from, before it was swallowed by the darkness of the night.

"Home run!" yelled Sean. "We're saved."

"I wouldn't be so sure," I said, keeping up the ferocious pace of my pedalling.

Puffing and panting, I continued to speed down the road, until we finally rounded the corner to Sean's street. I slammed on the brakes, while also grinding my runners into the floor, in order to stop sharply outside Sean's house. We jumped off the bike and dashed to the door and bolted inside. But as I went to shut the door, I saw, in front of the silvery moon, the silhouette of a bat. And it was heading our way!

Lockdown

I slammed the door behind us. He knew where we were. We had to keep him out.

"Quickly, shut all the windows," I ordered.

At once, Sean raced into the kitchen.

I ran over to the living room window and pulled it close, before lowering the handle to secure it. I could hear that Sean was still in the kitchen, so I took it upon myself to check the utility and the downstairs toilet. Both were open - the hot summer evening wasn't helping our current situation. Once I had finished, I found Sean back in the hallway and we raced up the stairs to secure the upstairs area. Sean did the bathroom and his bedroom and I did his Mum and Dad's room, before we met back on the landing.

"One room left," I said.

We opened the door to Mark's room and walked straight in.

"GET OUT!" Mark bellowed, over the deafening music that pumped out of the huge speakers that sat in the corner of the room. "How dare you. How dare you enter the room of, Deadly Nightshade!"

Sean ignored him and ran over to the stereo.

And when he turned off the music, Mark's face was one of utter shock. But that face was nothing compared to the one he pulled when Sean said, "We don't have time for your stupid music. This is important!" And then Sean said,

"The Orloks *are* vampires, Mark. We've just killed Cordelia with holy water and now Mr Orlok is after us. But the holy water is gone and we don't know how we are going to kill him now. And he's right outside. We just closed all the windows, but he'll try and get in, and if he does, we're all dead. DEAD! What are we going to do?"

Mark narrowed his eyes. "As if I am going to fall for that, "he said. "This is just your feeble attempt at payback for the trick I played on you yesterday, and it's pathetic. I can see right through it, you normos. Now, I'm going to count to ten and by then I expect the music to be back on and for you to be out of my room."

He started counting.

"One...two...three."

Mark didn't even get to four, before he was forced to stop.

"Hello, boys," came a sinister voice from downstairs. "Where are you? You know I'm going to find you."

"He's downstairs," I said. "How did he get in? We shut all the windows."

Sean put both of his hands over his face and shook his head. "Oh no, I forgot to shut the window in the kitchen."

"What do you mean you forgot? You were in the kitchen. What were you doing in there if you weren't closing the windows?"

Reaching into his pocket, Sean pulled out a handful of crumbly biscuits.

"I got distracted."

And then he said, "They're custard creams!"

As if that justified putting all our lives in grave danger!

Meanwhile, Mark had risen from his bed. He walked over to us, until he got really close, and he said, "So, you weren't joking? This is for real?"

We both nodded.

"What are we going to do?" he said, nibbling at his black fingernails.

"We hoped you would know," whispered Sean.

Mark shrugged his shoulders, hopelessly. And then his bottom lip began to tremble and he began to whimper. "I'm too young to die," he whined in a voice similar to that of an overly-tired toddler. "I've never even kissed a girl. And there's so much goth stuff I've yet to do."

But his babyish sniffling was interrupted by the sound of footsteps plodding up the stairs.

"Are you upstairs, boys?" asked Mr Orlok. "Wouldn't that be foolish? You would be trapped. At my mercy."

Then Sean and Mark did something. Something I'd imagine they hadn't done in a *very* long time. They hugged. And in this moment I knew that Mark was as useless as Sean and that it was once again, all up to me.

I looked around the room for inspiration. And that's when I saw Robert Smith looking at me sideways with one of his bearded dragon eyes.

Not by the Hair on my Chinny Chin Chin

We hadn't had long to discuss the plan. Only seconds. And the plan probably wouldn't even work. But while I was still terrified - terrified like you wouldn't believe - at least I had something to hold onto. A glimmer of hope. And, a focus.

I stood bolt upright in Mark's closet, Robert Smith nestled tightly in my arms. The smell of stale body odour from the rails upon rails of black t-shirts and jumpers sat strong in my nostrils. At any other time the smell would have been too strong, too overpowering, but under these circumstances, I would happily smell that putrid smell for the rest of my life, if only I could escape this predicament. I peered out of one of the slats of the wardrobe into the darkness of Mark's room. I could just about see Mark and Sean, who were under the bed, hiding.

Mr Orlok had now reached the top of the stairs. "Where are you boys? I'm going to find you," he called out. "I just need to decide which one of you to eat first."

We all remained deadly still and deathly quiet as we listened to the sound of Mr Orlok pacing around upstairs. We listened to him turn the doorknob of Sean's bedroom and enter the room. Then we heard him return to the hallway and go into Sean's parent's room. And then Mr Orlok's heavy footsteps approached the door of the room in which we hid. Suddenly, the footsteps ceased and everything fell silent for a moment. And then began a sinister rapping at the door.

"Little pigs, little pigs, let me come in," came the voice from the other side of the door.

The handle of the door turned slowly and the door creaked open.

I kept my eye pressed to the slit of the wardrobe and watched the dark imposing figure of Mr Orlok advance into the room.

"You know, we vampires are very good at seeing in the dark," said Mr Orlok. "We've evolved that way, you see. So I will find you, boys," he sneered.

It was time to put the plan in action. Very deliberately, I fidgeted around in the wardrobe. It worked.

Mr Orlok twisted his neck sharply and looked right in my direction.

"Oh, you're in the wardrobe," he said, gliding over.

My heart was beating out of my chest. I felt sick. And it wasn't the stench of Mark's wardrobe making me queasy - it was pure dread! But I was ready. I just hoped that Sean and Mark would do their part. And I prayed that it would work!

As Mr Orlok approached the wardrobe, I could see Mark and Sean quietly slide out from under the bed, behind him.

Mr Orlok reached out his hand and placed it on the wardrobe door handle. His burning red eyes were now all I could see through the narrow slat.

"Oh, O positive blood," he said, sniffing at the air like a bloodhound. "I *am* looking forward to this!"

Mr Orlok ripped open the wardrobe door.

And I cowered like a little lamb before the ferocious wolf stood over me.

Mr Orlok seemed to double in size before my very eyes. His shoulders hunched. His arms expanded. He was like a fierce and hungry dragon proudly spreading its wings. I knew that he was ready to pounce. Ready to devour me.

But Sean and Mark were ready, too. Each had two hands on the underside of Robert Smith's large reptile tank and had silently taken up a position right behind Mr Orlok. And then, just as Mr Orlok was about to strike, they heaved the tank up high in the air with all their might, before bringing it down, with an almighty crash, right on top of Mr Orlok's head. Glass shattered and cascaded to the floor. Robert Smith's water bowl fell out of the tank. A handful of half-chewed crickets, too. But Mr Orlok's head was still lodged very much inside.

"What's this," screamed Mr Orlok, as he tried to tug the huge tank from his head.

Meanwhile, Mark flung himself across the bedroom, like Indiana Jones, stretched out his arm and flicked on the switch of the plug at the base of the wall. Instantly, the UV tubes that lined Robert Smith's tank burst into fluorescent blue, bathing the room in an eerie violet glow.

"Arrrgh, turn it off!" Mr Orlok screeched.

We all watched as Mr Orlok began to tremble. This soon turned into a violent convulsion. Thin puffs of smoke then began coming out of his ears, then his nose, and finally, from behind his eyes. The smoke got thicker and darker, darker and thicker, and within no time at all, we could no longer see Mr Orlok's head any more through the black smoke that filled every inch of the reptile tank. Mr Orlok then started jerking wildly around on the floor, like a fish on the deck of a trawler, when all of a sudden, he burst into flames of brilliant blue. Turquoise fire engulfed his entire body. And then, as quickly as the fire had started, it stopped. Mr Orlok's charred body remained intact for a brief moment, before slowly collapsing into a huge pile of ash on the floor.

Sean looked at me and I looked at Sean. Neither of us spoke, but we each knew very well what the other was thinking - at last, it was over. We were finally safe.

Mark stood over the pile of ash. "You see what happens when you mess with Deadly Nightshade," he said, trying desperately to regain a measure of coolness that he had lost in bucketfuls during his earlier meltdown.

365 days - 52 weeks - a Year

That's how long it had been since that dramatic night last summer.

After the event we had obviously told our parents what had happened, who in turn informed the police. Of course, no-one had believed us at first, but over time people came to accept our story. After all, the evidence was there. Poor Miss Mangle's body was recovered, not from the garden of number 33, but from the attic of her very own house. And when the police checked the loft at Mr E. Wright's house, they found him, too. Both had bite marks on their necks. And that's when the forensic teams, who had been studying the Orloks' remains, came back with the results.

And everyone was amazed, because the scientists said that the Orloks' genetic makeup was unlike anything they had ever encountered before. A new species, apparently!

And then things got really intense! All these important people in suits interviewed us for weeks on end about the whole thing. We got such a grilling that I felt like a cheese toastie, at times. There were even two F.B.I agents sent over from America to talk to us. A stern woman with red hair and a funny chap who looked a bit like a moose and whose surname was Mouldy, or something like that. His first name was even funnier. Badger, was it? No - Fox!

And then, suddenly, it was all over the news. We found ourselves on the front of every newspaper and on every T.V channel across the land. We even got to be mascots at Old Trafford for a Manchester United match. The players said that we were heroes. Us! It was brilliant!

Of course, all this had made us quite famous. People would stop us in the street for pictures and autographs. I spent ages perfecting a cool signature. Sean didn't. He just wrote his name in his ordinary handwriting. But then he never wrote his proper name, Sean Smith. He always signed his name, Sean McCool.

Our fame and notoriety got so big that there had even been some official merchandise created with our faces on it and, 'Tom and

Sean - Vampire Hunters,' embellished on the side. There were t-shirts, water bottles, backpacks and lunchboxes. But while our Mums had bought some, they didn't sell well.

Anyway, I guess it is true what they say about everyone having their five minutes of fame. In fact, ours actually lasted a lot longer than five minutes, but, like everything, life goes on, people forget, and the past few months had seen life return to its normal ways. Not that there is anything wrong with normal, but after the dramatic events of last summer and what followed, I couldn't help but feel that this summer was dull and drab in comparison.

So, here I sat on the pavement, looking at the Orloks' still abandoned house, wondering if my life would ever again be touched by the same flicker of excitement.

And then I caught sight of Sean belting down the road.

"Tom, I've just been chatting to Mark," he panted, buckling over and placing his hands on his knees to catch his breath. "He said there's been strange going-ons. He said that since the new neighbours moved in to that house next to Hegarty's farm, loads of the animals have been killed. Eaten by a ferocious beast. Then, last night, when he went over there to check it out with Draven, he saw a hound. He said it was enormous. He said it made a St Bernard look like a poodle. He said....he said...."

"What did he say," I asked, impatiently.

"He said that he reckons the new neighbours are werewolves!"

I stood up. Maybe the new neighbours weren't as normal as they appeared to be? Maybe they were up to something? Maybe they were werewolves? Well, if they were, then they were messing in the wrong neighbourhood!

Thanks for reading.

I hope you enjoyed the book.

And if you did, please let your friends know.

Better still, get your teacher to buy a copy and read it to your class.

I would love as many people to read the book as possible, so spread the word.

And finally, if you did enjoy the book, then you would undoubtedly love my other book, Bolan: A Tyrannosaurus Pet, which you can purchase on Amazon.

Thanks, Sam.

The book has finished - what are you still doing here?